Pony-Crazed Princess

Princess Ellie's Treasure Hunt

by Diana Kimpton

Illustrated by Lizzie Finlay

Hyperion Paperbacks for Children / New York

AN IMPRINT OF DISNEY BOOK GROUP

For Alice and Thomas

First published in the United Kingdom in 2007 as
The Pony-Mad Princess: Princess Ellie's Secret Treasure Hunt
by Usborne Publishing Ltd.
Based on an original concept by Anne Finnis
Text copyright © 2007 by Diana Kimpton and Anne Finnis
Illustrations copyright © 2007 by Lizzie Finlay

Printed in the United States of America
First U.S. edition, 2008
1 3 5 7 9 10 8 6 4 2

This book is set in 14.5-point Nadine Normal.
ISBN 978-1-4231-1414-7
Visit www.hyperionbooksforchildren.com

Chapter 1

"Can I please stop now?" asked Princess Ellie.

"Certainly not," replied Miss Stringle. "Your vacation does not begin until class is over, and there is still half an hour to go."

"But John will be here soon," pleaded Ellie.

"No, he won't," said her teacher firmly. "Prince John is not due to arrive for another hour. Now, please get on with your work. Princesses should not argue."

Ellie sighed. She was tired of studying history. And she was tired of being in the palace library. She'd had enough of old books and ancient bookcases.

She longed to be out in the sunshine with her ponies. She glanced up at Miss Stringle. Maybe her governess would change her mind once she'd finished the work sheet.

The long list of questions was all about princesses from the past. Ellie had been working on them all afternoon. Thank goodness there were only three left.

She chewed the end of her pencil as she turned the gold-edged pages of *The Complete Guide to the Royal Family*. The huge book was packed with tons of

boring information. It said
when people were born
and when they died,
but it never mentioned
whether they liked ponies as
much as Ellie did.

She quickly discov-
ered that Princess Marissa's older brother
was called James and that Princess
Andromeda had married King Proctor the
Proud of Protavia. It took her much longer
to figure out that Princess Traviata was her
own great-great-great-great-aunt.

She wrote down the last answer and
waved her paper in the air. "I'm finished,"
she declared. "Can I stop now?"

"Not quite yet," replied her teacher.
She pointed at the books spread out in

front of Ellie. "I want you to put those back in their right places while I check your work. That way I can see if you've remembered what I taught you about how the library is organized."

Ellie groaned. She hadn't listened as Miss Stringle droned on and on about the library. She'd been too busy daydreaming about her five beautiful ponies. Now she had no idea where the books belonged.

She stacked them on top of one another, picked them up, and started to walk around the room. As she walked, she looked at the shelves carefully, searching for spaces that might give her a clue.

The first gap she spotted was high above her head. As she stood on tiptoe to push a book into it, the pile of books in her other hand started to wobble.

She tried to steady it, and she almost suc-
ceeded. But one book slid off. It tumbled to
the ground, slid across the shiny wooden
floor, and vanished under a bookcase.

Luckily, Miss Stringle didn't notice. She
was still busy checking the work sheet. Ellie

dumped the remaining books on a table. Then she got down on all fours and looked under the nearest set of shelves.

The book was all the way at the back, against the wall. She reached out to grab it and felt something long and soft brush against her fingers.

Ellie pulled her hand away in surprise. Then she peered under the bookcase again and spotted a piece of red ribbon dangling from the back of the bottom shelf. "I wonder how long that's been there," she murmured. The maids probably hadn't noticed it while they were sweeping.

This was much more interesting than her lesson. She forgot about the book for a moment and pulled gently on the ribbon. It didn't move. She pulled again, a bit harder.

This time it shifted a little and then got stuck.

Ellie gave it a short, sharp tug, and the ribbon finally pulled free. As it slid out of its hiding place, she saw for the first time that it was tied around a tightly rolled paper scroll.

"Princess Aurelia, what are you doing?" shouted Miss Stringle. "Get up at once! Princesses do not crawl on the floor."

"I'm sorry," said Ellie, wishing her teacher didn't insist on using her formal name. "I was just getting a book I dropped." She decided not to mention the scroll. That was her secret, and she wasn't ready to share it yet.

Chapter 2

Ellie grabbed hold of the book with one hand and the scroll with the other. Then she stood up very carefully and turned to face Miss Stringle. She held the book in front of her to distract her governess, but kept the paper hidden safely behind her back. If Miss Stringle didn't know it existed, she couldn't take it away or, worse, make Ellie write an essay about it.

Keeping her eyes fixed on her teacher, Ellie stepped sideways toward the table. Miss Stringle watched her curiously. "Why are you moving in such a peculiar way?" she asked.

Ellie's mind raced as she searched for a remotely believable reply. But before she could think of one, there was a loud knock on the library door. Miss Stringle looked around to see who was there, and Ellie quickly slid the scroll up her sleeve. She would have to wait until later to discover what was written on it.

Higginbottom, the butler, stepped into the library and gave a low bow. "I'm sorry to interrupt," he said, "but Prince John of Andirovia has arrived earlier than expected. He's waiting for Princess Aurelia to welcome him."

Ellie gave a whoop of delight. Although she e-mailed John all the time, she hadn't seen him since she and her parents had paid a royal visit to his parents' palace. "Can I stop now?" she asked Miss Stringle, for the third time. "Princesses should be polite to guests."

"That's true," agreed Miss Stringle, with a sigh. "I suppose you'd better go. And don't forget to have a good vacation."

"I won't," cried Ellie, as she rushed out of the library. She expected to find her friend waiting for her outside. But he wasn't there. The corridor was empty.

The butler winked at her and smiled. "Prince John thought you might like an excuse to get out of class," he explained. "He's gone straight to the blue guest room to change into his riding clothes. He'll meet you at the stable."

"Brilliant," said Ellie. John was just as

pony-crazed as she was. It was going to be wonderful having him stay at the palace for a few weeks.

She raced up the spiral stairs to her very pink bedroom, took off her frilly pink dress, and put on her pink jodhpurs. As she slid her feet into her new pink riding boots, she remembered the scroll. She hadn't wanted to tell Miss Stringle about it, but her friends were different. It would be fun to share the secret with them.

Ellie picked up her dress from the floor and pulled the roll of paper out of the sleeve. She stared at it for a moment, eager to discover what was written inside. Then she quickly ran down to the stable to meet John, clutching the scroll safely in her hand.

When Ellie reached the yard, she found

her best friend already there. Kate, the cook's granddaughter, was home early from school, and she was busy grooming her brown-and-white foal, Angel.

Before they had time to speak, John ran into the yard carrying a long cardboard box. "Look at this!" he cried, as he waved the box at the two girls. "It's my latest gadget. I only got it this morning, so I couldn't resist bringing it with me." He knelt down and started pulling off the sticky tape that held the box shut.

Ellie was too excited about her own news to wait for him. "I have something to show you, too. But it's a secret. You've both got to promise not to tell."

She waited impatiently until the others had agreed. Then she held out the scroll and explained, "I found this during my history lesson. It was hidden behind the books in the library."

"It looks really old," said Kate. "See, the ribbon's faded."

"And the paper's yellow with age," said Ellie.

"Old things aren't always very interesting," said John. "It might just be a blank piece of paper, or a shopping list."

For a second or two, his words made Ellie doubt her own enthusiasm. Then she remembered where she'd found the scroll. "No one would go through such trouble to hide a shopping list," she declared. She pulled the ribbon loose. Then she carefully started to unravel the scroll, holding it out so the others could see it.

The paper wasn't blank. There was old-fashioned writing on it that was hard to read. There were several squiggly lines, too, and drawings of trees.

"It's a map!" cried John. "Those squiggles mean a stream, and those two lines over there mean a bridge."

Kate pointed at a large cross. "It's telling us where to find something. But what?"

Ellie's hands shook with excitement as she revealed the last part of the scroll. The writing at the top was in capital letters. They spelled out a single word.

"Treasure!" cried Ellie, Kate, and John in unison.

Chapter 3

"Wow!" said John. "I've never seen a real treasure map before."

"Look at the date!" cried Kate. "It's a hundred years old."

"That's even older than Great-Aunt Edwina," laughed Ellie. Then she peered at the strange writing and started to read out loud: *"Go to the place north of the stream where three oak trees grow. Start by the tree*

that's closest to the palace. *Walk ten paces toward the west, and start to dig. My treasure is hidden in the ground.*"

"That's perfect," said John. "Now you've *got* to be interested in my gadget. It's just what we need." He ripped open the box he was carrying and pulled out a metal circle attached to a long handle.

"That's a funny-looking spade," laughed Kate.

John gave a superior smile. "It's not a spade. It's a metal detector. It will help us find exactly the right place to dig."

"But what if the treasure's not metal?" asked Kate.

"But it must be," John insisted. "We're really

18

close to the sea, so it must be pirates' treasure, and pirates always bury gold!"

"I'm not so sure," said Ellie. "It could have been buried by a princess who wanted to hide all her rubies and diamonds and emeralds."

"Or it could be a whole lot of paper money buried by a millionaire," suggested Kate.

"Oh," sighed John, his voice tinged with disappointment. "My metal detector's not going to find any of those things." Then he thought for a moment and grinned. "But it *will* find the treasure chest. Treasure chests always have metal hinges."

At that moment, Angel nudged John's arm so hard that he nearly fell over. Then she started to paw the ground with one of her front hooves.

Kate laughed. "She's tired of standing still. She's not as excited by treasure as we are."

"Shadow would be, if the treasure were a stash of peppermints," said Ellie. They were her Shetland pony's favorite sweets.

John patted the foal's neck. "She's grown since I last saw her. Is she big enough to ride yet?"

"No," said Kate. "It will still be a long time before she's strong enough. She's only a baby."

"And she still likes to stay close to her mom," added Ellie. "She likes to follow behind if one of us is riding Starlight."

At the mention of her name, the bay mare put her head over the door of a nearby stall and whickered gently. Angel whickered back and reached out her nose to nuzzle her mother.

"Why don't we go for a ride with them now?" suggested John. "We could try to find those oak trees."

"Which trees?" asked Meg, the palace groom, as she carried a bulging hay net into the yard.

Ellie hesitated. She wanted to keep the map secret, so she could find the treasure with her friends. She didn't want her parents to take over. They would probably make Higginbottom dig the hole for her with a silver spade. But she hated the idea of lying to Meg.

Luckily, John was good at talking his way out of problems. "Ellie found a drawing in the library with some trees on it," he said. It was the perfect reply. It gave just enough information, but not too much.

Ellie followed his lead. "We're going to look for the place where the trees grow."

"And we're going to take Starlight and Angel," added Kate.

"Have a lovely time, then," said Meg. "But don't go too fast, and stay out of the woods. You don't want Angel getting lost or left behind."

It didn't take them long to decide which of Ellie's five ponies they would ride. Kate wanted Starlight, so she could be close to Angel. John chose Sundance, the chestnut, because he was the same color as John's two ponies at home. The final decision was

Ellie's, and she picked Rainbow, her gray Welsh pony.

They put on the ponies' saddles and bridles and rode out of the yard toward the deer park. As they went up the path, they chatted excitedly about the treasure. There were so many things it could be and so many people who could have buried it. But John remained convinced that it was pirates' gold.

As they expected, Angel kept close to Starlight. Then they passed the paddock where Ellie's other two ponies were enjoying a rest in the shade. Shadow was busy eating, as usual. Moonbeam, the palomino, cantered toward them and stood with her head over the fence.

Angel couldn't resist saying hello. She trotted over to her friend, and they sniffed each other's noses. Starlight whinnied after her, obviously worried that her baby had gone too far away. Angel whinnied a reply and trotted back to join the group.

As soon as they reached the deer park, the ponies started to jog and pull on their reins. They could feel the grass beneath their feet and wanted to go faster. Ellie knew they needed to use up some energy, but she remembered Meg's warning. "We'd better not gallop with Angel," she said to the others. "Let's canter instead."

She let the gray pony trot for a few steps. Then she sat down in the saddle and squeezed her legs against Rainbow's sides. The pony obediently broke into a steady canter—not too fast and not too slow. Ellie relaxed in the saddle. Cantering was so comfortable. It always reminded her of riding her old rocking horse.

Kate and John rode beside her, matching Rainbow's pace. Angel kept up easily. Her legs were thin and spindly, but they were nearly as long as Starlight's. She was obviously enjoying herself. She tossed her head

with delight as her hooves pounded the grass.

They cantered across the corner of the deer park toward the stream. When they were nearly there, they slowed the ponies to a walk. "Let's look for those trees," said Ellie.

"There's a weeping willow over there," said Kate, pointing at a large tree on the opposite bank. Its branches drooped lazily down into the water.

"That's no good," said John. "It's on the wrong side of the stream, and it's the wrong kind of tree. We're only interested in oaks."

"There aren't any here," said Ellie. The banks of the stream were covered with grass and wildflowers. The willow was the only tree close to the water.

"The ones on the map were farther away

from the stream," said John. "We'd better investigate those over there." He waved his arm in the direction of several groups of trees that dotted the open parkland.

As they walked the ponies toward the closest group, Starlight whinnied again. Angel had fallen behind. She was still by the stream, busy sniffing the bushes and tasting the wildflowers.

The foal squealed in response to her mom's call and cantered over to her. But she didn't stop. She sped on, lifting her back legs in a playful buck as she went. She reached the trees, then spun around and galloped back.

"She's not keeping as close to her mom as I'd expected," said John.

Ellie watched anxiously as Angel galloped

away again. "She's getting more confident all the time," she said. "She didn't run around like this last time we took her out."

"I wish she wasn't doing it today," said Kate, as the foal hurtled in between the trees. "Where's she gone now?"

Starlight whinnied for her again, but this time there was no reply.

Angel had completely disappeared.

Chapter 4

"Oh, no!" said Ellie. "Meg told us to keep Angel out of the woods."

"It's not really the woods," said John. "It's just a few trees growing close together." But he looked worried, too.

They trotted over to where they had last seen the foal. Ellie's stomach was in a knot. Suppose Angel had gotten hurt? Her spindly legs could break so easily.

Suddenly there was a loud crashing sound in the undergrowth, and the brown-and-white foal raced out in front of them. Rainbow was so surprised that she jumped sideways. But Ellie didn't mind. She was just glad that Angel was all right. "I think we should keep away from the trees from now on," she said.

"I think so, too," agreed Kate. "It's not a safe place for a foal."

"But we need to look at the trees if we're going to find the treasure," said John. "I'm dying to find out what it is."

"Angel's more important," said Ellie firmly. "We'll have to come back tomorrow without her." She turned Rainbow around and headed back toward the stable.

Kate and John turned Starlight and

Sundance, too. Angel followed close behind. As they rode, John looked up at the sky. "Would your dad lend us a helicopter?" he asked. "My parents have three, and they are always happy to let me use one."

Ellie sighed. John was very good at persuading the Emperor and Empress of Andirovia to let him have his own way. She had much more trouble with the King and Queen. "Dad's only got one," she admitted, "and he's not likely to let us have that."

"Anyway, we'd have to tell him why we wanted it," added Kate. "I thought this was supposed to be a secret, so we could look for the treasure by ourselves."

"It is," said John, "but it would be so

much easier to spot the right trees if we had a helicopter. From the air we could see everything laid out just like it is on the map."

To Ellie's relief, they managed to get back to the stable without losing Angel again. The foal still wandered off from time to time when she saw something interesting to explore. But there were no more trees, so she never went out of sight.

Just as they reached the yard, Ellie had an idea. "There is another way to get up high," she said, pointing at the palace. "The corner towers are really tall. We'll get a fantastic view of the grounds if we climb up to the top of one."

"Great idea," said Kate.

John grinned. "We'll have time to do it before dinner if we hurry."

They unsaddled the ponies as quickly as they could and settled them in their stalls with fresh water and plenty of hay. Then they ran back to their rooms to change out of their riding clothes before they went exploring.

Ten minutes later, they met at the bottom of the West Tower. Ellie was the last to arrive. She found the others sitting on the stairs waiting for her. "Sorry I'm late," she said. "I went back for my binoculars."

"I brought mine, too," said John, holding up a much bigger pair. "They're explorer grade, with digital focusing, tinted lenses, and—"

"Tell us later," interrupted Ellie. "We need to get started. It's an awfully long way to the top."

The spiral stairs were covered with soft, red carpeting that muffled the sound of their footsteps. The walls were lined with paintings of Ellie's relatives.

Kate looked at the pictures anxiously as

she climbed the steps. "I wish their eyes weren't following me," she said.

"They're not. It's just an optical illusion," said John. He stopped to look at a painting of a man in old-fashioned clothes holding an elaborate brass object with lots of knobs. "Wow! Look at that gadget! I wish I had one like that."

"I'd love a tiara with golden horseshoes on it, just like hers," said Ellie, pointing at a picture of a girl and a boy dressed in royal clothes. "I wonder if she's one of the princesses I was learning about today. I remember Princess Marissa having a brother."

"Whoever she was, I think she was as pony-crazed as we are," laughed Kate. She climbed another step and stared at a painting of a man on a horse. "Tiaras aren't really my thing. I'd much rather have a white stallion like his."

"He'd be too big for you," said John. "You'd have to wait until you were grown up to ride him."

"When I grow up, I'm going to have my own stable," said Kate.

"I'm going to have seven horses," said John. "One for each day of the week."

"And I'm going to put an elevator in this tower," added Ellie. "My legs are so tired."

The higher they climbed, the steeper the stairs became. The carpet stopped at the fourth floor. After that, the steps were just bare wood, and the handrail was merely a piece of rope screwed to the wall.

Ellie held the rope tightly as she climbed.

She hoped desperately that her plan was going to work. All this effort would be worthwhile if it helped them find the hidden treasure. But what if they couldn't spot the right trees when they reached the top?

Chapter 5

At long last, Ellie and her friends reached the top of the stairs and stepped out into a circular room with brick walls. They paused for a moment to catch their breath. Then they ran over to the only window and peered out.

Ellie was right. The view was fantastic. They could see the palace grounds spread out beneath them.

"Look how blue the sea is," said John,

pointing at the distant horizon.

"And look at all those trees," groaned Kate. "How are we going to tell which are the ones near the treasure?"

"The map will help," said Ellie. She spread it out on the windowsill so that they could all see.

"There's the stream," said John, pointing at the wiggly lines on the paper.

"And there it is outside," said Kate. "You can see the sun reflecting off the water."

John looked at the map again. "It doesn't show the whole stream. Just the part near the bridge. So that's what we should look for."

"Which bridge?" asked Kate. "There are two of them."

"Hmm," said John. "I can't tell which one it is on the map."

"But I know," said Ellie. "One of them's quite new. I had to cut the ribbon at the opening ceremony when I was four. So it wasn't here a hundred years ago."

"Which one was that?" asked John.

It took Ellie a little while to spot it. "It's over there," she shouted, as she pointed out

40

through the window. "Now, let's find those trees."

Ellie peered through her binoculars, looking carefully at the groups of trees that dotted the palace grounds. From her high vantage point, she soon realized that several of the clusters were too big. They con-tained far too many trees. Some of the others weren't close enough to the stream.

"Those might be the ones," she said, pointing at a group of trees not far from the bridge.

"And so could those over there," said John, pointing at another group. "But I think those are the only two groups of trees that might be the ones on the map."

"I agree," said Ellie. "The treasure must be beside one of them." A shiver of excitement ran down her spine as she gazed out the window. "It's just sitting there in the ground, waiting for us to find it."

"I wish we could look for it now!" cried Kate.

"So do I," said John.

"But we can't," said Ellie. "We'll get into trouble if we're late for dinner." She turned around and sighed. "And we've still got to go down all those stairs again."

Ellie met Kate and John at the stable the next morning, right after breakfast. Ellie had the map. Kate had two spades that she'd borrowed from her grandfather, and John had his metal detector.

"It's a good thing it's got a superdeluxe folding handle," he said. "Otherwise, it wouldn't fit in my backpack."

"I wish the spades had them, too," groaned Kate. "Their handles stick out the top of my backpack."

They groomed the ponies quickly and put on their saddles and bridles. Then they mounted and set off toward the stream. Ellie led the way on Rainbow. John was riding Sundance again, but Kate had Moonbeam this time. They'd decided it was safer to leave Starlight at home with Angel.

The first group of trees they reached was the one by the bend in the stream. As soon as they arrived, John jumped down from his saddle and started to unpack his metal detector.

There were three trees, just like on the map, and they were all enormous. Ellie rode Rainbow in between them and stared up at the mass of green leaves that shut out the sun. Then she noticed something.

"We're in the wrong place!" she shouted to the others. "These aren't oaks."

"How do you know?" said John, as he unfolded the superdeluxe handle of the metal detector. "They're big enough to be oaks."

"But they've got the wrong kind of leaves," said Ellie.

Kate rode up beside her and looked carefully at the trees. "Ellie's right," she agreed. "Oak leaves have wigglier edges. I learned about them in school."

"Come on," said Ellie, "let's try the other place."

John looked longingly at his metal detector. "Maybe I should just try it out while we're here," he suggested.

"No!" shouted Ellie and Kate in unison.

John sighed and put the gadget back in his backpack. Then he swung himself into Sundance's saddle, and they rode on toward the other clump of trees they'd spotted from the tower.

Ellie's stomach was churning with nerves. Surely this must be the right place, she thought. If it wasn't, there would be nowhere else left to look for the treasure.

Chapter 6

As soon as Ellie, Kate, and John arrived at the other group of trees, they saw that they were indeed oaks. But they weren't alone. There were several smaller trees growing around them.

"Does that mean we're in the wrong place again?" asked Kate. "The map doesn't say anything about other trees."

"But the map was drawn a hundred years

ago," said John. "Those smaller trees are much younger than that. They wouldn't have been here then."

Ellie grinned. "Let's get started," she said. "I'm ready to find that treasure."

They tied the ponies to the trees with the halters they'd brought with them. Then Ellie pulled out the map and looked at the instructions again. "We've got to start by the oak closest to the palace," she said.

"That's that one over there," said Kate.

They walked over to it and squeezed through the brambles and bracken to reach the trunk. "Now, take ten paces to the west," read Ellie.

"Wait a minute," said John. He rummaged in his backpack and pulled out a small black gadget. "It's my new, explorer-grade compass. It tells you the time, the date, *and* your height above sea level."

"But does it tell you which way's west?" asked Kate.

"Of course it does," replied John. He looked at the gadget. Then he pointed into the distance and said, "It's that way."

"Great," said Ellie. "Now, all together: ten paces forward."

"One, two, three . . ." they counted as they slowly stepped forward in the direction John had indicated. But when they reached "ten," they found they weren't all in the same place. Kate was farthest back. Ellie was a little way ahead of her, and John was well out in front.

"Oh, dear," said Ellie. "We've all taken different-size steps. How can we know which of us is right?"

"John's definitely wrong," said Kate. "He took ridiculously big steps."

John folded his arms and sighed. "That's because I was pretending to be a pirate. Pirates always have long legs."

"Short pirates don't," argued Kate.

"It doesn't matter, anyway," said Ellie. "We don't even know for sure that this is pirates' treasure. It could have been buried by someone else."

"Someone who takes small steps, like me," said Kate.

"Or someone who takes big steps, like me," said John.

"Or any size steps in between," said Ellie. "The treasure could be hidden anywhere between the two of you."

John grinned. "Now you know why we need my metal detector. Let's put sticks in the ground to mark our positions. Then I'll know where to search."

He pulled the gadget out of his backpack and unfolded the superdeluxe handle. Then he started to swing the metal detector slowly from side to side, keeping the bottom of it close to the ground.

Ellie and Kate watched anxiously. They didn't have to wait long for something to happen. After only a few seconds, the machine started to beep loudly.

John pointed triumphantly at the ring on the bottom of the instrument. "I've found it!" he yelled. "The treasure's under here."

Ellie and Kate grabbed the spades and started to dig. Luckily, the ground was quite soft, but digging was still hard work. There were so many roots in the way. Suddenly, Ellie's spade clinked against something hard.

"There's something here!" she yelled. She knelt down and scrabbled in the soil with her fingers. But all she found was an old metal bottle cap. "That's not it," she said, as she threw it off to the side in disgust.

John waved the metal detector over it. The machine beeped in exactly the same way it had before. Then he waved it over the hole and there was silence. "Sorry," he said, as his ears turned pink with embarrassment.

"False alarm. There's nothing else there."

He started to search again, walking slowly back toward the oaks. For a long time, he worked in silence. Then the metal detector started beeping again.

"I hope this really is the treasure," said Ellie, as she and Kate started to dig some more. But it wasn't. This time all they found was a rusty nail.

Kate gave an exaggerated yawn. "That's even less exciting than the bottle cap."

"No, it's not," said John, looking at it carefully. "This isn't just any old nail. It's a nail from a horseshoe. You can tell by its shape."

"But it's still not treasure," said Ellie.

"I'm sure we'll find the real thing soon," said John, as he started to search again. But he sounded slightly less confident than he had before.

"I hope we won't have to dig too many more holes," said Kate. "I'm getting tired."

"So am I," said Ellie. "Let's take a rest."

They wandered back to the grove of trees and checked to see that the ponies were all right. Then they sat down on a tree stump and watched John wave the metal detector back and forth.

After a while, Ellie got bored and looked around at where she was sitting. There were

some leafy twigs sticking out of the side of the stump. What was left of the tree was trying to grow again.

Ellie stared at the twigs in alarm. Then she nudged Kate urgently with her elbow. "What kind of leaves are those down there?" she asked, pointing at the twigs.

"Oak, I think," replied Kate.

"I think so, too," said Ellie. She jumped to

her feet and looked closely at the stump. "This tree had a much wider trunk than the other oaks, so it must have been older. That means there were *four* oaks here a hundred years ago, not three."

Kate's shoulders slumped in despair. "No wonder we haven't found the treasure. We're in the wrong place."

"But there's nowhere else to look," groaned Ellie. "There's no way we're going to find the treasure now."

Chapter 7

They took the long way home to cheer themselves up. It was fun jumping over logs in the woods and galloping through the deer park. But even that didn't take away their disappointment.

"Are you sure there's nowhere else to look?" asked Kate, as they clattered into the yard.

"Definitely," said John. He jumped down

from Sundance's back and patted the chestnut pony's neck. "Those were the only groups of trees in the right place. The map must be referring to a different palace."

Ellie thoughtfully twisted a strand of Rainbow's mane around her fingers. "It doesn't make sense. Why would anyone hide a map of someplace else in our library?"

John and Kate both shrugged their shoulders. None of them knew the answer to that question. All they knew was that they'd failed. The excitement of the treasure hunt was over.

They unsaddled the ponies and set them loose in the paddock with Starlight and Angel. Then they hung the halters up in the tack room and walked miserably out of the yard. There was no point in wondering what kind of treasure it was now. It didn't matter anymore. They weren't going to find it.

They were halfway back to the palace when they encountered an old lady in a long skirt. "Dear me!" she said. "I'm sure children didn't look that gloomy when I was a girl."

The sight of her favorite great-aunt cheered Ellie up a little. She smiled weakly and said, "I didn't know you were coming for a visit."

"Neither did I, until this morning," replied Great-Aunt Edwina. "That's when I decided I couldn't stand the chaos at home any longer. The construction workers have made such a mess. There's dust everywhere and muddy footprints all over the floor."

Ellie gave a playful smile. "I suppose it was never like that when you were a girl," she said, echoing her great-aunt's favorite complaint.

Great-Aunt Edwina burst out laughing. "Actually it was much worse then. You should have seen all the mess here when your great-grandfather landscaped the palace grounds. The whole place looked like a construction site."

"I wish I'd seen it," said John. "I love bulldozers and diggers and cranes."

"I'm not sure they had all of those," said the old lady. "But they had lots of men with shovels. They laid the gravel driveway, dug the fishpond, moved the bridge, and built the wall around the kitchen garden."

Ellie, Kate, and John stared at her,

openmouthed in astonishment. Kate was the first to recover sufficiently to speak. "Did you say they moved the bridge?"

"Yes, my dear," said Great-Aunt Edwina.

"So, a hundred years ago, it must have been in a different place," said Ellie. Her earlier disappointment had been replaced by a glimmer of hope.

"Of course it was," replied Great-Aunt Edwina.

"Where?" asked Ellie, Kate, and John in unison.

The old lady gazed thoughtfully up at the sky as if she expected to find the answer written in it. "I think it was farther west," she said. Then she looked doubtful and added, "Or was it farther east?"

"Can't you remember?" pleaded Kate.

Great-Aunt Edwina shook her head sadly. "I'm afraid not. My memory is not as good as it was when I was a girl." Then she looked at her watch and tut-tutted to herself. "Now I'll have to say good-bye. I've asked Higginbottom to bring me some tea and cake on the lawn." She turned and walked away toward the palace garden.

Ellie waited until she was out of earshot. Then she said, "It's a good thing she didn't ask why we were so interested in the bridge."

"But it's a shame she couldn't tell us where it used to be," grumbled John.

Kate nodded. "I wonder how we can find out?" she asked.

Suddenly, a pony started to whinny loudly. It wasn't a happy sound. There was an edge of fear to it. A shiver ran down Ellie's back as

she realized she'd heard it before, on yester-
day's ride.

"It's Starlight!" she yelled, as she ran
toward the paddock. "There must be something wrong with Angel."

Kate's face was white as she raced beside
Ellie. John was close behind them, and, in
the distance, Ellie could see Meg running
from the stable. She must have heard
Starlight, too.

They found the bay mare on the far side of the paddock. She was cantering up and down along the fence, calling loudly for her baby. Sundance, Rainbow, and Moonbeam were watching her. But there was no sign of Angel.

"She must have gotten out," said Meg. "But I don't see how. I checked the fence myself this morning."

"Maybe she crawled out underneath," suggested John.

Kate shook her head and sniffed back a tear. "I don't think she could. The bottom rail's too low."

Suddenly, Ellie noticed that one of the fence posts was leaning over slightly. It was standing next to a tree, and between the two was a tiny gap. Ellie pointed at it and asked,

"Could Angel have gotten through there?"

Meg ran over and examined the spot. "She must have pushed the post over with her rump," she said, pointing at some strands of brown-and-white hair caught in the wood. "The space is just big enough for her to wriggle through. But it's too small for Starlight to follow."

Kate stared anxiously over the fence. "She could be anywhere on the grounds by now."

"Don't worry," said Ellie. "We'll find her." But deep inside, she didn't feel as confident as she sounded. She hoped the foal's curiosity hadn't gotten her into real trouble this time.

Chapter 8

John squeezed through the gap in the fence and looked carefully at the ground. Then he shook his head. "I can't see any hoofprints. They don't show up on this springy grass."

"Oh, no!" groaned Kate. "That means we have no idea which way she went."

"But we know she's not anywhere we can see from here," said Ellie. "That rules out all the open grassland."

"We'd better split up and start searching," said Meg. "You come with me, Kate. We'll look down toward the stream. Ellie, you go with John and search farther north."

Ellie wriggled through the gap in the fence and raced off with John in the direction Meg had pointed. There were several clumps of trees over there. Perhaps Angel was hiding in one of them.

The first group of trees was small. It was easy to see that Angel wasn't there. The second was much bigger. They had to go in between the trees to check. The leafy branches intertwined above their heads, shutting out the sunlight. Elle was thankful that Angel wasn't brown all over. It would be easy to spot her white patches in the dark.

Minutes ticked by while they searched

every possible place the pony could have been. "She's not here," said John at last.

"We'd better try somewhere else," said Ellie. She ran out into the sunlight again and headed for the next group of trees. "Angel!" she called as she ran up to it. "Where are you, Angel?"

To her delight, she heard a faint whinny in response. John heard it, too. They both stopped, hoping the foal would run out and surprise them, as she had on the previous day.

But she didn't. She just whinnied again, louder this time and more urgently. "She's frightened," said Ellie, as she ran toward the cluster of trees. John raced close beside her.

They had to force their way through the thick undergrowth. Prickles tore at their clothes and scratched their hands. But Ellie didn't care. Saving Angel was worth a few scratches.

They found the foal trapped in a dense patch of brambles. The strong stems were wound around her legs. Her neck was damp with sweat from her efforts to free herself. But the more she struggled, the more entangled she became.

"You're all right now," said Ellie in a soothing voice. "We'll get you out of there soon." She bent down and tugged hard on one of the stems, trying to pull it away from Angel.

The foal flinched and squealed in pain. A trickle of blood ran down her leg where a sharp thorn had dug into her skin.

"I'm sorry," said Ellie, fighting back the tears that filled her eyes. The last thing she'd wanted to do was hurt Angel even more.

"We can't pull the brambles off," said John. "We'll have to cut her free."

Ellie's eyes lit up. "Great," she said. "You must have a knife in your survival kit."

"Of course I do," said John. "It's an explorer-grade camping knife with twenty-four different functions." Then his ears

71

turned pink again. "Trouble is, I didn't bring it with me. It's back at the stable, in my backpack."

Ellie groaned. There was nothing else they could do by themselves. "We've got to get help," she said. "But we can't leave Angel here on her own. She might panic."

"I'll go," said John. "You stay behind. Angel knows you better than me." He spun around and raced off toward the stable.

The foal snorted in alarm at the sudden movement. She started to struggle again, trying to pull herself free from the brambles. Ellie knew she had to stop her. If she didn't, Angel might snap one of her spindly legs.

Chapter 9

"Steady, Angel," said Ellie, trying hard not to let her own fear show. "You've got to stand still, or you might hurt yourself really badly."

To Ellie's relief, the sound of her voice made the foal relax. Angel flicked her ears forward and stopped struggling against the brambles. But as soon as Ellie stopped speaking, the frightened foal resumed her fight to break free.

So Ellie started talking again, saying the first things that came into her head. She told Angel how beautiful she was and how John would be back soon with help to cut her free. She told her about the treasure and how they didn't know where to look for it. And all the time she was speaking, Angel stood still and listened.

It didn't matter what Ellie said. It was the sound of the words that mattered—not their meaning. She rambled on and on. When she started to run out of things to say, she looked around her for inspiration.

"That's an oak tree over there," she said. "You can tell, because the leaves have wiggly edges. That's another oak over there, and that other tree's an oak, too.

"Look how big they are," she continued,

as she glanced around to see what else she could talk about. "They're much older than you. They must have been here for years and years and years."

She paused and licked her lips. They were dry from talking so much. But Angel didn't like the silence. She snorted and started to struggle again.

"Please don't do that," said Ellie, stroking the foal's face. "I promise I won't stop again." As she spoke she looked out through the trees at the open ground in front of them. She could see Kate, John, and Meg running across the grass. Help was nearly there, but she knew she had to keep talking until it arrived.

"See the stream right over there, Angel? There's a bridge that goes over it, but we can't see it from here. It's too far away." As she was speaking, she spotted two identical mounds close together on the bank of the stream. "Look at those," she told Angel. "They're much too square to be natural. And there are matching mounds on the opposite bank. I bet they're all that's left of the old bridge!"

At that moment, John raced up, with Kate and Meg close behind. "I've brought my

76

knife this time," he said, as he pulled it out of his backpack.

"And Meg borrowed shears from the gardener," said Kate. She patted Angel's neck and slipped a halter over her brown-and-white nose. "I'm not going to let you run away again," she told the pony, as she fastened the strap behind Angel's ears.

"We've got to keep talking," explained Ellie. "It keeps her calm."

So they chattered about what they were doing as they worked to free the trapped foal. First Meg and John cut through the twisting stems. Then Kate and Ellie helped them pull the vicious thorns away from Angel's legs and body. Their own hands and arms were soon covered with scratches, but nobody complained.

When the foal was finally free, Meg ran
her fingers over Angel's legs and body, feel-
ing for injuries. "Now make her walk away
from me, Kate," she said. "And then make
her trot. I need to see if her legs are okay."

Ellie held her breath, hardly daring to
look. This was the real test. This would
show if Angel had hurt herself badly.

The foal stepped forward cautiously, as if

she weren't sure she could move without pain. But her confidence grew with each step. Soon, she was walking normally, putting her weight evenly on each leg. When Kate asked her to trot, she managed it easily without any sign of limping.

"Thank goodness for that," said Meg. "She's a very lucky pony. She's escaped with nothing more than a few small cuts."

"That's amazing," said John.

"I'm so relieved," said Kate, as she hugged Angel in delight.

Ellie just grinned. She'd done enough talking for a while.

Meg pulled her first-aid kit from Kate's backpack and started treating Angel's wounds. Kate held the foal still, while John and Ellie acted as assistants, passing the cotton wool and antiseptic powder when Meg requested it.

Eventually, Meg straightened up and smiled. "She'll be fine now. I'm so glad everything's turned out well in the end."

"Not quite everything," said John. "We still haven't found the—"

Kate kicked him in the ankle before he could finish. "That's supposed to be a secret," she hissed.

"What is?" laughed Meg. "I love secrets, and I'm very good at keeping them. You should know that by now."

"That's true," said Ellie. "So I suppose it doesn't matter if you know about the treasure."

"Especially since we don't know where it is," said Kate.

Ellie laughed. "Actually, I think I do," she said.

Chapter 10

Everyone stared at Ellie. "How come you know more than us?" asked Kate.

"Because I spotted the site of the old bridge while I was waiting with Angel," explained Ellie. She pointed toward the strange mounds beside the stream. "It's just over there, which means these three oaks are in exactly the right place."

"Awesome!" yelled John, pulling his

metal detector out of his backpack. "I'm all ready. Let's go."

Meg held Angel while Ellie, Kate, and John looked for the oak tree closest to the palace. Just as before, John used his compass to find which way was west. Just as before, they all walked forward ten paces, and, just as before, they all ended up in different places.

John pulled out his metal detector, unfolded the superdeluxe handle, and started to search. Ellie watched him anxiously. Her fists were clenched so tightly that her fingernails dug into the palms of her hands.

Suddenly, the metal detector started to beep loudly.

"Here's the spot!" yelled John. "And the signal's really strong. Whatever's down there is much bigger than anything we've found before."

Ellie and Kate grabbed the spades and started to dig. Soon there was a pile of dirt beside them and a large hole nearly two feet deep.

"Are you sure this is the right place?" said Ellie, as she paused for a rest.

"Of course I am," said John. "I'll show you." He put the metal detector into the hole, and it beeped even louder than before.

The sound gave Ellie hope. She thrust her spade into the bottom of the hole as hard as she could and hit something solid. With a squeal of delight, she started to scrape away the dirt to see what it was.

Kate helped, and so did John. They didn't find a bottle cap or a horseshoe nail this time.

They uncovered a metal box.

John helped Ellie lift it out and put it on the grass. "Look at that rust," he said. "It's been underground for a really long time."

"A hundred years, we hope," said Ellie.

"Shall I open it?" said John.

"No," said Kate. "Let Ellie do it. She found the map, and she's the one who found the right place to dig."

Ellie knelt down in front of the box, while everyone else crowded around to watch. Her

stomach was churning with nerves. She couldn't bear the thought of another disappointment. Hardly daring to breathe, she swung the lid open and peered inside.

At the bottom of the box lay a strange collection of objects. There was a painting in a fancy frame, a horseshoe, a braid made of long gray hair, a letter, and something wrapped in red cloth.

Kate was bouncing up and down in excitement. "What does the letter say?"

"Is it from a pirate?" asked John.

Ellie picked up the paper and unfolded it. The handwriting was the same as on the map. *"Congratulations,"* she read out loud. *"You have found my treasure. My name is Princess Marissa. I buried this box on my tenth birthday. I love my pony, Tinkerbelle,* more than anything else in the whole world, so most of the things I treasure have to do with her. The horseshoe is hers, the braid is made from hairs from her tail, and the painting shows how beautiful she is."

Ellie stopped reading and picked up the picture. It showed a girl riding side-saddle on a gray pony.

"Tinkerbelle looks just like Rainbow," said Meg.

"And Marissa looks like the princess in that paint-ing in the tower," said John. "I wonder if that's a picture of her."

"This painting's much better than that one," said Kate. "I think it's gorgeous."

"Then you can have it," said Ellie, pushing it into her hands. "We all found the treasure, so we should all share it."

"That sounds fair," said John. "But what does the rest of the letter say?"

Ellie started reading aloud again. *"My brother, James, helped me dig the hole and bury the treasure. He's put in the penknife he got for Christmas."*

"Oh, it's not there anymore," said John, in a disappointed voice.

"Yes, it is," said Meg. "I can just see the end of it sticking out from under that red cloth."

John reached into the box and pulled out the penknife. A line of tiny diamonds made the letter *J* on the polished wooden handle.

"I told you there'd be jewels," laughed Ellie.

"*J* for James and *J* for John," said Kate. "That's definitely for you to keep."

Ellie agreed. Then she read the last part of the letter. *"There is one other thing here that is not Tinkerbelle's. Unwrap the cloth to find out what it is."*

"Go on, Ellie," said John.

"We've both got something already," said Kate. "Whatever's in there must be for you."

Ellie picked up the mysterious bundle and unwrapped it carefully. As the red cloth fell away, the sunlight glittered on a beautiful tiara decorated with golden horseshoes.

"It's the one from the painting!" gasped Ellie.

"I told *you* there'd be gold," laughed John.

"And I told you that that princess was pony-crazed," said Kate.

Meg took the tiara and placed it gently on Ellie's curly hair. "That couldn't be a better fit," she said. "It's a present from one pony-crazed princess to another."

John pulled a camera from his backpack. "We should get a picture of us all with the treasure," he said.

"I'll take it," said Meg.

"We have to include Angel," said Ellie. "We would never have found it without her."

They all crowded around the foal, with the

treasure box on the ground in front of them.

"Smile," said Meg, and she pressed the button.

"Brilliant!" said Ellie. "That picture's going to be the first thing I put in my own treasure box. Who knows, maybe another pony-crazed princess will find it a hundred years from now."

Collect all the adventures of Princess Ellie!

Join Ellie as she goes exploring, solves mysteries, and, of course, spends as much time with her ponies as possible!